THE LAST BOOK BEFORE BEDTIME

NICOLA O'BYRNE

nosy crow

AT THE END OF A DAY that's been filled with lovely things that ping and beep and buzz and glow, there's nothing better than one last-book-before-bed.

You could say it's the most important story of the **whole** day. But which story will it be?

Um . . . hello? Three Little Pigs, can you hear me?

I SAID . . . what could the last-book-before-bed possibly be?!

Please excuse us, we seem to be having some technical difficulties.

ONCE UPON A TIME, there were Three Little Pigs. When they were all grown-up, their mother sent them out into the world to seek their fortunes, but first she kissed them on their piggy noses and said, "Work hard, and remember – beware of the

BIG BAD WOLF!"

The Three Little Pigs soon found a meadow where
the flowers smelled so lovely, and the river bubbled
so cheerfully, that the First Little Pig declared,
"This meadow is perfect! I shall build my house
right here, and I shall make it out of straw!"

Well, we all
know how
THAT'S going
to turn out.

But before the First Little Pig could even start
building his house, there was a rather pink interruption.

It was Cinderella.

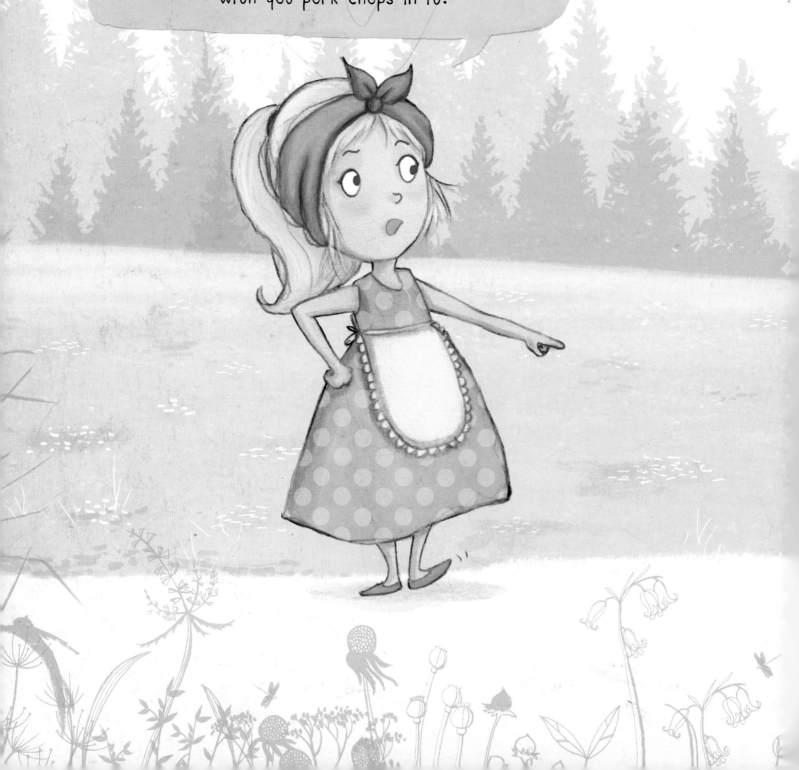

If this is the last storybook before bedtime, you really want a PRINCESS story. My book has romance, an evil stepmother and everyone knows princess stories are made into films and toys. No one's going to want to watch a film with you pork chops in it.

Well, you're here now Cinderella. Let's see what happens . . .

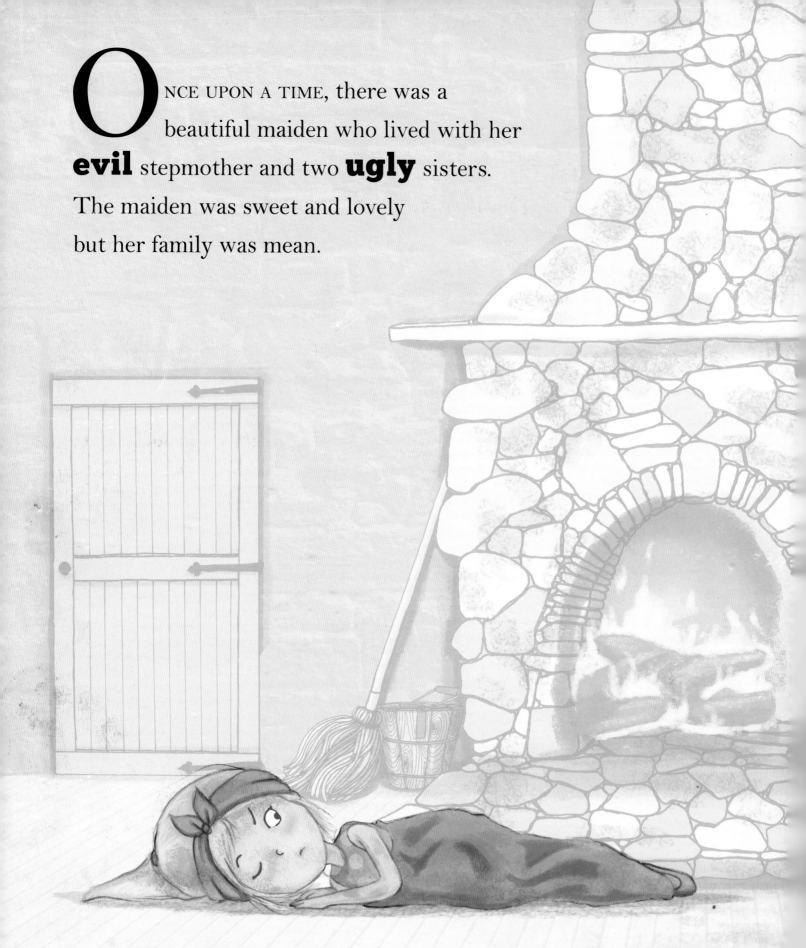

ONCE UPON A TIME, there was a beautiful maiden who lived with her **evil** stepmother and two **ugly** sisters. The maiden was sweet and lovely but her family was mean.

They made her sleep by the fireplace and, because she was always covered in cinders, they called her Cinderella.

One day, an invitation arrived from the Royal Palace.
The Prince was holding a grand ball and everyone
was invited! Everyone, that is, except Cinderella.
Her **evil** stepmother would **NOT** let her go.

Hang on, is this
a kissy-kissy
story now?

Who cares?!
There's a banquet
in this story.

I'd just like to point out
that there are no pigs in
the "Cinderella" story.

Settle down, Little Pigs. You three can be the **evil** stepmother
and the **ugly** stepsisters. Right, Pigs! Get your dresses on!

As the Three Little Pigs – sorry, the **evil** stepmother and the **ugly** stepsisters – left the house, Cinderella began to cry, for she desperately wanted to go to the ball, too.

Suddenly, there was a puff of magic and a fairy appeared!

We shall go to the ball!

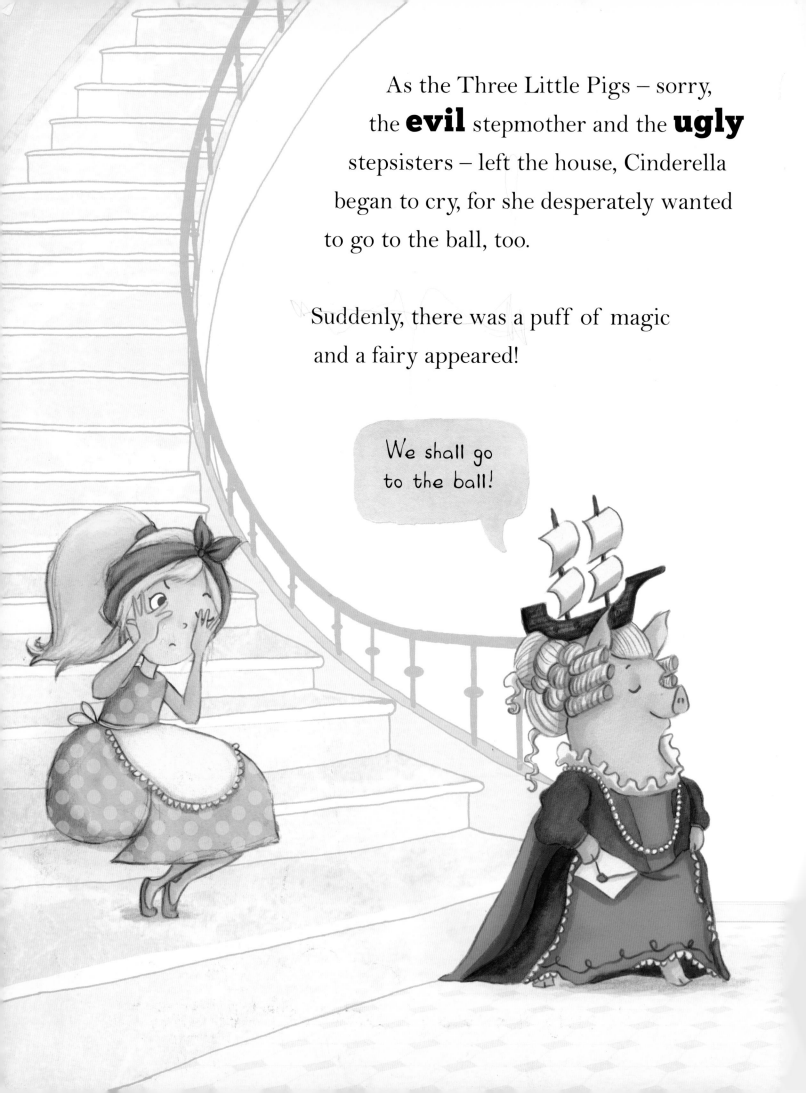

I said . . . A FAIRY APPEARED!

Well, this is embarrassing.

It usually works. Let's try again.

But who's going to be the fairy?

I'm just looking forward to the cake.

Suddenly, there was a **PUFF of MAGIC** and . . .

. . . Little Red Riding Hood and the Big Bad Wolf appeared?! That's a surprise!

Listen, the Fairy Godmother can't make it. Ignore all this fancy princess stuff - the last storybook should be exciting, and full of action and danger. I'm way more interesting than the "Cinderella" story.

Did I miss anything?

Well, now that you're both here,
let's get back to the story.

Everyone settle down! Let's try again.
Cinderella, you can be Little Red's mother. Pig number two,
you're the granny. And Wolf, you're not in this bit.

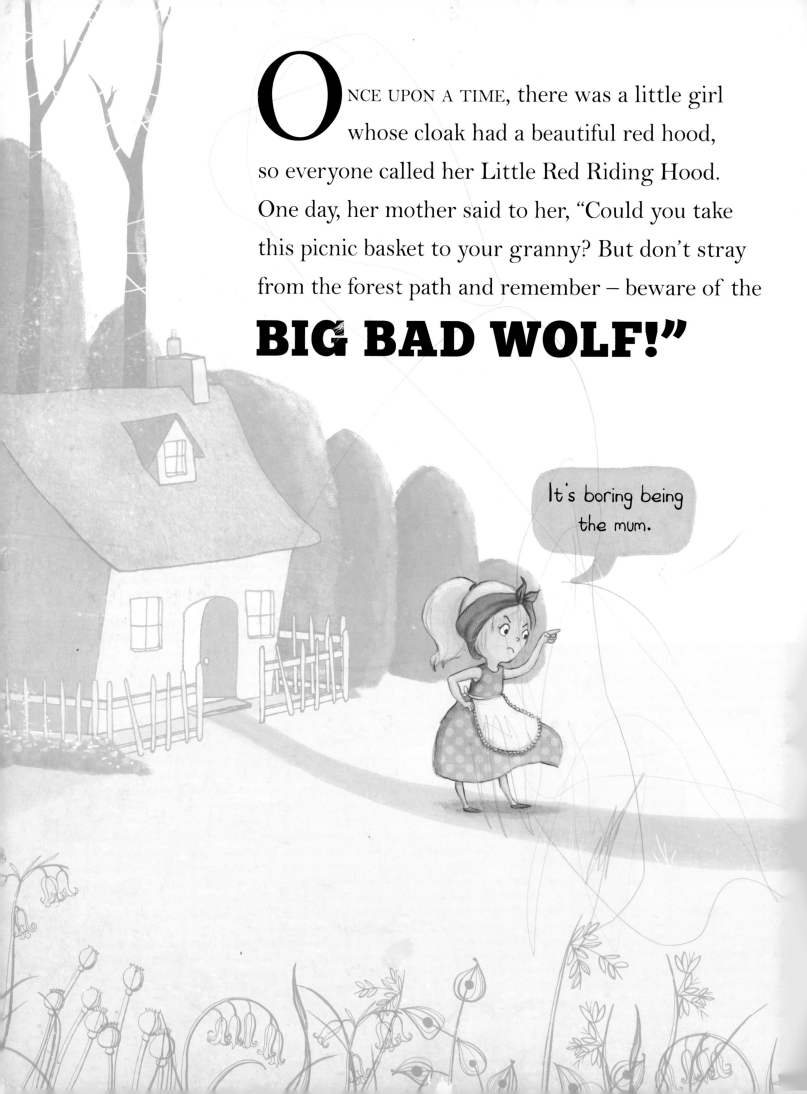

Once upon a time, there was a little girl whose cloak had a beautiful red hood, so everyone called her Little Red Riding Hood. One day, her mother said to her, "Could you take this picnic basket to your granny? But don't stray from the forest path and remember – beware of the

BIG BAD WOLF!"

It's boring being the mum.

Little Red Riding Hood was skipping along,
when who should she meet but the Big Bad Wolf?
"Good morning, Little Red Riding Hood," he said.
"Where are you off to so early and all by yourself?"

"I'm off to see my poor, sick granny
and take her some of my mother's elderflower
cordial and cake," replied Little Red Riding Hood.

Everyone, quiet down! You're ruining the story! And be careful! Don't you know that books are only made of paper?!

THIS IS RIDICULOUS! If I can't be the star of the story, then NOBODY can! I'm going to pull this book to pieces!

I was promised cake!

Huh! Two can play at that game, Cinderella. You can't always be the centre of attention!

. . . rip the

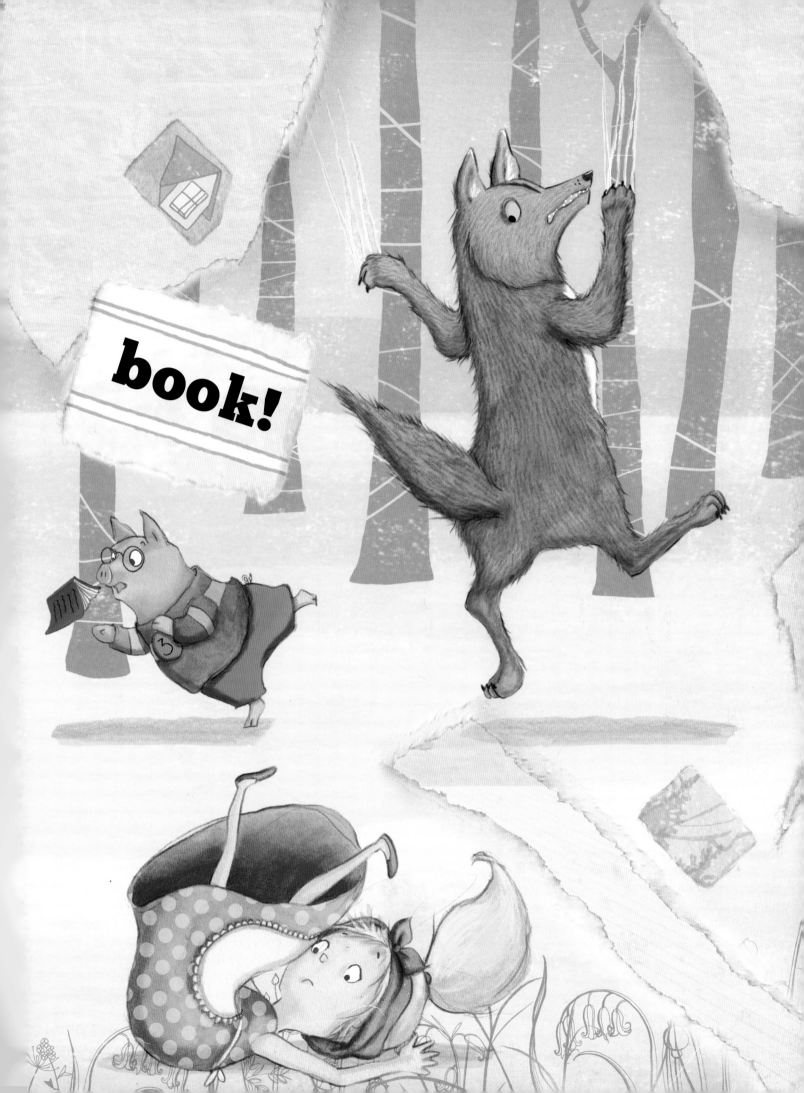

book!

OH NO! The book's in pieces!

And now it's bedtime and we have **NO** story.

Whatever are we going to do?

ONCE UPON A TIME, there were Three Little Pigs.
They were hard-working and resourceful,
and lived in a beautiful brick house in a lovely location.
On this particular day, they were hosting tea and cake
for their friends, Little Red Riding Hood and Cinderella.

Just then, Little Red Riding Hood arrived.

"Cinderella's just texted me," she said.

"She's not feeling well and won't be able to come to tea."

"Then we shall go to her!" cried the Third Little Pig,
who was not only handsome but kind and good.
So they packed up all of the lovely food and drink
and set off for Cinderella's house.

The path to Cinderella's house
wound through a deep, dark forest
and who should they meet there
but the Big Bad Wolf?

The Three Little Pigs and Little Red Riding Hood
were afraid of wolves and decided not to stop
and talk, but this wolf saw the picnic basket
and guessed where they were going.

"I'm going to sneak to Cinderella's house first,"
thought the wolf, "and when they arrive,
I'll **gobble** them up!"

When the Three Little Pigs and Little Red Riding Hood arrived at Cinderella's house, they found SOMEONE in bed – SOMEONE who was wearing Cinderella's favourite pink scarf.

"What big **eyes** you have," said Little Red Riding Hood.

"All the better to see you with!" said the SOMEONE.

"What big **ears** you have," said Little Red Riding Hood.

"All the better to hear you with," said the SOMEONE.

The Third Little Pig looked at the SOMEONE very carefully.

"What big **teeth** you have," said the Third Little Pig.

"All the better to . . .

. . . EAT YOU WITH!"

shouted the Big Bad Wolf,
and he leapt out of bed.

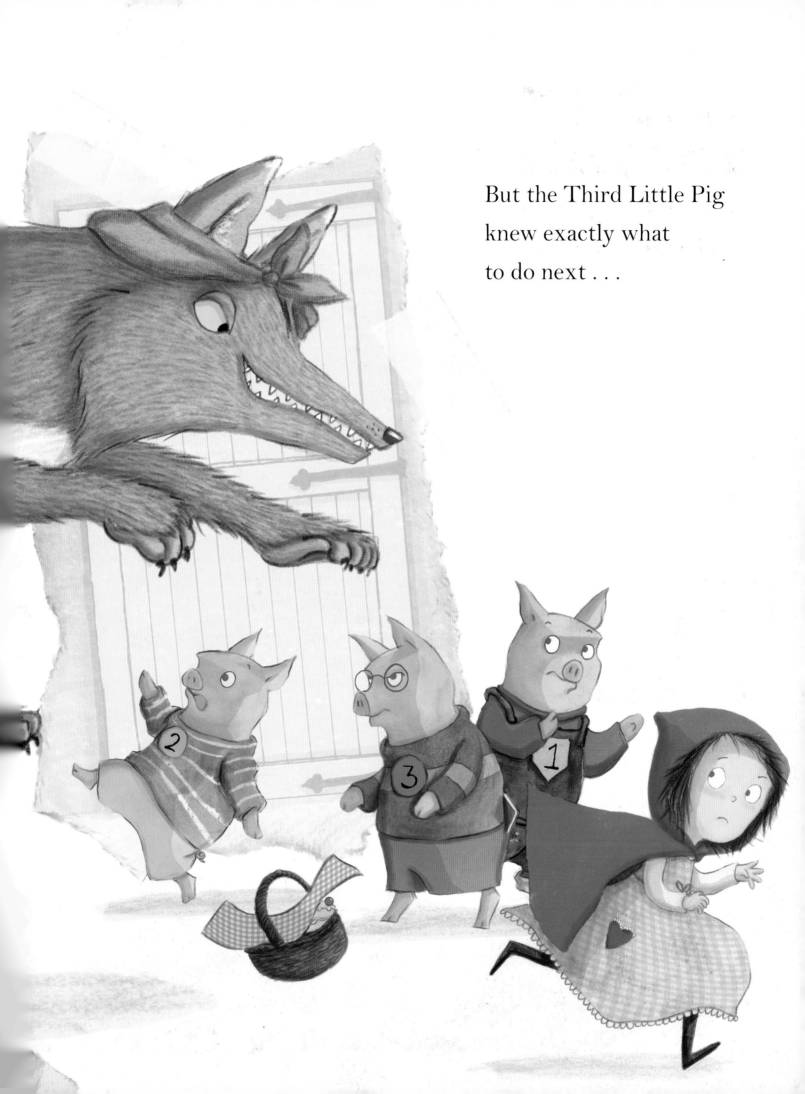

But the Third Little Pig
knew exactly what
to do next . . .

. . . he leapt forward and wedged a large slice
of cake firmly into the Wolf's huge, toothy mouth.
"IT'S SO DELICIOUS!" cried the Wolf.
"Even tastier than little pigs or little girls!"

The First Little Pig then let
Cinderella out of the cupboard,
where she promptly fell in love
with him.

But they didn't kiss
because this isn't
THAT kind of story.

And they all lived happily ever after.

Well done, team! You did a great job in the end!

That was just what a last-book-before-bed should be.

Are you still awake?! Oh, no!

But we've run out of pages!

We're going to need another book!

Which book are **you** going to choose?